PUFFIN BOOKS

THE ROMAN BEANFEAST

Gillian Cross worked in a school and a bakery before studying at Oxford and Sussex universities. She has also been a childminder and an assistant to an MP. She has written around thirty books for children, many of them published in Puffin. In 1991 she was awarded the Carnegie Medal for *Wolf* and has won both the Smarties Prize and the Whitbread Award for *The Great Elephant Chase*. Gillian Cross lives in Warwickshire with her husband and two of their four children. Her hobbies are orienteering and playing the piano.

Other books by Gillian Cross

THE DEMON HEADMASTER
THE PRIME MINISTER'S BRAIN
THE REVENGE OF THE DEMON HEADMASTER
THE DEMON HEADMASTER STRIKES AGAIN
THE DEMON HEADMSTER TAKES OVER

THE GREAT ELEPHANT CHASE
NEW WORLD
ON THE EDGE
PICTURES IN THE DARK
RENT-A-GENIUS
TWIN AND SUPER-TWIN
WOLF

For older readers

TIGHTROPE

GILLIAN CROSS

THE ROMAN BEANFEAST

Illustrated by Linzi Henry

PUFFIN BOOKS

To Jenny Cessford, whose class had the invasion, and Liz Watts, who showed me the onagers. Thank you for teaching my children about the Romans.

PUFFIN BOOKS

Published by the Penguin Group
Penguin Books Ltd, 80 Strand, London WC2R 0RL, England
Penguin Putnam Inc., 375 Hudson Street, New York, New York 10014, USA
Penguin Books Australia Ltd, 250 Camberwell Road, Camberwell, Victoria 3124, Australia
Penguin Books Canada Ltd, 10 Alcorn Avenue, Toronto, Ontario, Canada M4V 3B2
Penguin Books India (P) Ltd, 11 Community Centre, Panchsheel Park, New Delhi – 110 017, India
Penguin Books (NZ) Ltd, Cnr Rosedale and Airborne Roads, Albany, Auckland, New Zealand
Penguin Books (South Africa) (Pty) Ltd, 24 Sturdee Avenue, Rosebank 2196, South Africa

Penguin Books Ltd, Registered Offices: 80 Strand, London WC2R 0RL England

www.penguin.com

First published by Hamish Hamilton Ltd 1996
Published in Puffin Books 1997
This edition has been produced exclusively for Nestlé Cheerios and
Honey Nut Cheerios 2003
3

Filmset in Baskerville

Printed in England by Mackays of Chatham Ltd, Chatham, Kent

British Library Cataloguing in Publication Data
A CIP catalogue record for this book is available from the British Library

ISBN 0–141–31670–5

1. Ask Molly

"YOU WANT TO win the *rhubarb pies*?" Dad said. His voice came scratchily down the phone from India. He sounded very far away.

"Not the rhubarb pies!" Davey shouted. "The *Roman prize*. We've all got to make something for our Roman project. We're going to choose the winner when we have our Roman feast at the end. What can I make?"

"*I* don't know," Dad said. "Why don't you ask Molly next door?"

Davey sighed. That was what people had always said, ever since he and

Molly started going to school. *Ask Molly*. Just because she never forgot anything, and she always knew what to say. Did they think he couldn't manage on his own? Did they think he *liked* being bossed around?

"But Molly wants to win the prize herself, Dad –"

The phone crackled. "Sorry . . ." Dad said, ". . . can't hear . . . ask Molly . . . Bye."

"Bye." Davey put the phone down and sighed again.

His mother came rattling down the stairs, with a wriggling twin under each arm and a blue bag of jumble on her wrist.

"Get down!" shrieked Luke.

"Down!" yelled Sarah.

"Not on your life," Mum said. She dropped the jumble, pushed Luke into one side of the double-buggy and

strapped him in with one hand. Then
she dumped Sarah beside Luke. "Did
you have a nice talk to Dad?"

Davey pulled a face. "I wanted to tell
him more about our trip to the Roman
fort, but the phone was too crackly."

"Never mind," Mum said. "He'll
phone again soon. When is the trip,
anyway?"

Davey's mouth fell open. Had she
forgotten? "It's –"

But before he could tell her, there

was a knock on the front door. Molly was standing primly on the doorstep, holding her pink lunch box.

"Have you got your packed lunch, Davey?" she said. "And your money for the trip?"

Davey's mum froze. "Trip?" she said.

"Didn't Davey tell you?" Molly's eyes widened. "We're going to the Roman fort today."

There was a loud yelp. "Davey! Why didn't you remind me? Where's the letter about it? With the form, to say you can go?"

"You put it in the airing cupboard to dry," Davey said. "After you washed Sarah's yoghurt off it."

Mum shrieked and raced upstairs. Sarah and Luke began to yell.

"Yog!"

"Want yog *now*!"

Molly shook her head. "Honestly,

Davey. You'd forget everything, if I didn't remind you."

"I *didn't* forget –"

Davey's mum came racing down again and fell over the blue bag of jumble at the bottom of the stairs. "Go on without us, Molly," she said, dashing into the kitchen.

"It's all right. I'll wait." Molly peered into the kitchen, watching Davey's mum cut thick slices of bread. "I've got salmon sandwiches and kiwi fruit. What's Davey having?"

There was no answer. Davey hoped Mum was putting *something* inside his sandwiches. She didn't always remember.

Two minutes later, Mum ran out of the kitchen, pushing the lunch into a blue plastic bag. She dumped the bag beside the buggy and snatched up her purse.

"Here's your form, Davey. And have I got five pounds? Yes – just!" She gave him the money and grabbed the blue bag from the bottom of the stairs. "Come on. Hurry!"

When they got to school, the coach was already there. Mum thrust the blue bag into Davey's hand.

"Have a good time."

"Don't worry," Molly said. "I'll look after him."

She pushed Davey into a front seat and slipped in beside him. Davey would rather have sat with Garry, or Jason, but he couldn't move without making a fuss, so he stared out of the window until they arrived at the fort.

When they got there, Mrs Johnson produced a bundle of quiz sheets. "Go round and find out the answers to these. Keep the partners you've been sitting with. And watch out for things to make for the Roman prize."

Molly jumped up. "Come on, Davey!" She bounced off the coach and ran towards the entrance of the fort.

Davey got stuck behind everyone else. By the time he climbed out of the coach, Molly was already at the main gate, scribbling the first answer on to the quiz sheet.

"We're supposed to be doing that together," Davey said.

"We are doing it together," Molly said. "You're just slow."

She ran through the gate, looking for the next answer and when Davey caught up, she was writing again. He looked over her shoulder, to read the

question, but she whisked the paper
away.

"Wait! I'll tell you the next thing
when I've written this."

They finished long before everyone
else. Molly tucked the clipboard under
her arm and grinned smugly.

"Let's go and spend our money."

"Money?" Davey said. "I gave my money to Mrs Johnson."

"That was your *trip* money, dummy." Molly pushed him towards the building labelled *Museum and Shop*. "Didn't you bring any extra money for souvenirs? My mum gave me two pounds."

Davey shook his head.

"Well, look round the museum then." Molly elbowed him through the door. "Try and find some good ideas for the Roman prize." She headed for the counter.

Davey was left standing beside a model of the fort as it used to be. He crouched down to look at it. There were tiny men playing games and cooking their dinner in cauldrons. And a wooden catapult, as big as a cannon, for throwing rocks at enemies in a battle.

10

Maybe he could make a model of that for the prize . . .

He studied the catapult until his leg began to go to sleep. Then he stood up and took a step backwards.

Right on to someone's foot.

"Sorry," he muttered.

There was a loud giggle from the counter. "You are a *dummy*!" Molly said. "Who d'you think you're talking to?"

Davey turned round. The person behind him wasn't a person at all. It was a life-size model of a tall Roman soldier with a funny little mouth and bushy eyebrows. And a very big red nose.

"Julius Sneezer!" Davey said, before he could stop himself.

Molly giggled again. "You dummy. You're talking to a *model*!"

"I'm *not*!"

It was too late. "Hey, everyone!" Molly shouted. "Look at Davey's new friend! He's found another dummy!"

There was an explosion of sniggers. Whirling round, Davey saw the rest of the class standing in the doorway. Laughing at him.

Mrs Johnson clapped her hands. "I don't know what's so funny, but you can stop giggling. It's time to fetch your packed lunches from the coach."

"Come on," said Molly. She dragged Davey to the coach and picked up his blue bag. "It doesn't feel as if *you've* got much."

It didn't look like much, either. Davey took the bag and opened it. It wasn't much. Mum had picked up the wrong bag. *She'd left his lunch and given him the jumble!*

He tried to hide it, but Molly's hand dived into the bag.

"Look, everyone! Look what Davey's got for lunch!"

And she pulled out a huge brown T-shirt with a hole in.

2. The Onager

NEXT TIME DAD phoned it was from Singapore. "How was the Roman fort?"

Davey wasn't going to tell anyone about the T-shirt. Mum knew about his lunch being left at home, but not about the jumble bag. He'd hidden it right at the back of his wardrobe.

"Well?" said Dad. "Did you see anything to make for the rhubarb pies?"

"There was a machine for throwing rocks."

"A machine for *sewing socks*?"

14

"Not socks," Davey said. *"Rocks!* Like a giant catapult."

"I know," said Dad. "An onager. That would be a good thing to make. Can you manage it before that feast of yours?"

Davey frowned. "If I can remember it well enough. Have we got a picture of one?"

"I don't think so. Maybe Molly has. She's got lots of books."

"I don't want to ask Molly –"

But the phone went funny. Suddenly Dad wasn't there any more. Davey put the receiver down and went into the kitchen. Luke and Sarah were having their tea, and Mum had spaghetti hoops on her jumper and grated cheese in her hair.

"Have we got any wood?" Davey said.

Mum frowned. "I don't think so. Perhaps Molly has."

"I don't want to ask Molly –"

Too late. Just at that moment, Molly walked past, on her way back from the shop. Davey's mum pushed the window open.

"Molly dear, have you got any wood? Davey needs some to make a – to make a *what*, Davey?"

Davey hung his head. "One of those catapults at the Roman fort," he muttered.

"Oh!" said Molly. "You mean an *onager*." She looked hard at Davey. "Is it for the Roman prize?"

"Maybe," Davey said carefully.

Molly gave a bright smile. "I've got lots of wood. Come round!"

She took Davey into the shed and found some bits of wood and a handful of nails. And she showed him the picture of the onager in her encyclopaedia.

But only for one minute. Then she snapped the book shut and tucked it under her arm. "That's enough," she said. "I've got something important to do now."

She pushed Davey out and slammed the door after him. As he went home, he heard her go back into the shed and start hammering. *That's funny*, he thought. *What can she be making?* But he

didn't have time to worry about it. He
went into his garage and began to sort
out the wood she'd given him.

None of it was quite the right shape.
And he couldn't remember the picture
properly, because he hadn't seen it for
long enough. But maybe he could
make a sort of onager, almost as big
as a real one, if he nailed that long bit

of wood *there*. And the little bit across the top . . .

He worked for two hours. When his mother came to find him, he was just fixing the last piece of wood.

"Wow!" said Mum. "Is that it?"

Davey nodded. "Can I take it to school tomorrow?"

"Take it to *school*?" Mum gulped. "I suppose so. We'll balance it on the buggy, and Luke and Sarah can take turns to walk."

It wasn't easy. Mum had to push the buggy with one hand and hold on to a twin with the other. And Davey had to walk bent double, to stop the onager falling out of the buggy seat.

Luke and Sarah thought it was wonderful.

"Dayday!" gurgled Luke, who was in the buggy. Opening his mouth, he took out a piece of toast, left over

from breakfast, and squashed it into Davey's ear.

"*My* Dayee!" screeched Sarah. She tottered over and pulled Davey's hair. He wouldn't have minded, but her hands were covered in porridge. By the time they got to school, he needed a bath.

He heaved the onager off the buggy. "Thanks, Mum."

"Are you sure you can manage?" his mother said anxiously.

"I'll be fine," Davey said. Why did she always treat him as if he was two? "Bye, Mum."

He staggered off, with the onager in his arms. It was so big he couldn't see round it. By the time he reached the door, he had bumped into five people and three trees, and his arms were aching. But he managed to stumble down the corridor to his classroom.

As he tottered in, he heard Mrs Johnson gasp.

"What a wonderful onager!"

Davey grinned and put it down. "Thank you."

Then he realized that she wasn't talking to him at all. She was looking at another wooden model, on the other side of the room. It was twice the size of his, and it looked *exactly* like the onager in Molly's encyclopaedia.

Molly was standing beside it, with a grin all over her face.

"It's nothing." She caught sight of Davey and grinned even harder. "Hallo, dummy! You've got porridge in your hair."

Davey scowled at her. Then he looked at Mrs Johnson. "*I* made an onager too."

"So you did!" Mrs Johnson said

brightly. "Very nice, dear. Maybe next time you'll have an idea of your own."

"It *was* my idea," Davey muttered.

But no one noticed, because Molly came sailing across the room. She grabbed the rock-throwing arm of Davey's model. "Does this onager work?"

"Let go!" said Davey. "It doesn't –"

But Molly ignored him. With a heave, she tugged the arm backwards. It snapped off at the bottom, and she was left holding a long piece of wood, with a little piece nailed across the top.

"Oh dear!" she said pathetically. As if she wanted to cry.

Mrs Johnson patted her shoulder. "Never mind, dear. Accidents will happen. Davey can take it home and mend it, can't you, Davey?"

Davey nodded, crossly. But he knew he couldn't take the whole onager, because Molly's mum was fetching him, and she wouldn't have a buggy. All he could carry was the broken piece of wood.

He took that home, hoping there would be something to fix on the bottom, so that he could join it all up

at school next day. But he couldn't
find anything.

   He ended up hiding the wood in his
wardrobe, right at the back. Next to
the bag with the brown T-shirt.

   He would have to think of
something else to make.

3. The Fly Blind

"YOU COULD MAKE a fly blind," Dad said.

At least, that was what Davey heard. The phone was even more crackly this time. Dad was phoning from Fiji.

"Who wants a blind fly?" Davey said.

"I said a *fly blind*!" Dad shouted. "*You* know! A strip of paper with us at one end and the Romans at the other. And ten centimetres for every hundred years in between."

Suddenly it all made sense. "Oh," said Davey. "You mean a *time-line*!"

"That's what I said." His father's voice faded for a moment. When it came back, he was saying, " . . . you could look up lots of dates in the library."

"Oh yes!" Davey grinned. "I could do the Second World War, and the Vikings, and the first car, and –"

"And Henry the Eighth, and the Battle of Hastings, and –"

Glug! The phone went dead. Davey waited, but Dad didn't come back, so he put the receiver down and raced up to the bathroom.

"Mum! I want to go to the library!"

Mum was washing Weetabix off Luke's ears. "We-ell –"

"Libey!" Sarah's eyes lit up. "Me *like* libey!"

"Books!" said Luke. He hit Sarah with the flannel.

Mum pulled a face. "We'll go after

school. But we can't stay long. You know what the twins are like."

"I'll be like lightning!" Davey said.

But lightning wasn't fast enough. The moment they arrived at the library, Luke and Sarah raced across to the picture book box. They began to pull out all the books and hurl them on the floor.

Davey grabbed an encyclopaedia

and began to scribble down dates. *William the Conqueror – 1066 . . . Second World War – 1939-1945 . . . First man on the moon – 1968.*

While Mum put the picture books back, the twins charged off in opposite directions, heading for the shelves. The librarian chased Luke, and Mum ran after Sarah.

And Davey leafed frantically through the encyclopaedia. *Guy Fawkes – 1605 . . . first postage stamp – 1840.*

"We'll have to go!" Mum called. She tucked Sarah under one arm as the librarian cornered Luke.

"One more minute," Davey said. "Please!"

"No – now!" Mum said. "Or something terrible will happen."

It did. Luke dived at a book spinner and sent it crashing to the floor. Books showered everywhere.

"Oh dear!" said a voice from the library door. "Luke and Sarah *are* being naughty, aren't they?"

It was Molly, with her father.

Davey's mother waved to them as she grabbed Luke. "Come on, Davey. We're going *now*. You'll have to make your time-line with what you've got."

Molly's eyes gleamed. "Is Davey making a time-line?"

Davey saw her peering at his bits of

paper as he scooped them off the
table and hurried after Mum.

He spent the whole evening working
on the time-line. He cut out a thin
strip of brown wrapping paper, three
metres long, and measured it into ten
centimetre lengths. Then he wrote
down all the dates he'd looked up, in
the right places on the line. There
were almost enough.

As he coiled it up, Mum came down

from bathing the twins. She smiled. "Mrs Johnson's going to be really pleased."

"Mmm." But Davey had a nasty feeling that she wasn't going to be pleased with *him*.

Molly came round next morning with a huge coil of paper, as big as a cartwheel.

"Mrs Johnson is going to love this!" she said.

Davey didn't say anything, but he pushed his time-line into his pocket before Molly noticed it.

Mrs Johnson went quite pale when she saw what Molly had brought. "It's huge! What is it?"

"It's a time-line," Molly said proudly. "It goes back two thousand years! Look!"

"There may not be enough room –" Mrs Johnson began.

But Molly was already undoing the
end of the roll. NOW, it said, in big
black letters. She pushed it into
Davey's hands.

"Hold this while I unroll the rest."

"Wait –" Mrs Johnson said.

But Molly didn't wait. She began to
walk backwards, slowly unrolling the
paper. As she went, Davey could see

things written on it. *Birth of Molly James . . . Birth of Mrs James . . . Birth of Mr James . . . Birth of Grandma James . . .*

By that time, Molly had reached the window, but she wasn't put off. "Hold this, Garry," she said. "I'm going outside."

Before Mrs Johnson could stop her, she ran out of the classroom and appeared on the other side of the window, tapping on the glass. Garry

undid the catch and she took the roll of paper and began to move backwards across the playground. Back and back and back . . .

For the first few metres, Davey could still read things on the paper. *Queen Victoria dies . . . the Great Exhibition . . . the Railway Age . . .* Then Molly got too far away.

When she was half across the playground, the other children began slipping outside, to cheer her on. Mrs Johnson had to go out too, to keep them quiet, and Davey was left on his own.

Stuck.

He was still holding his end of the paper – the end that said NOW – while the other children walked further and further back into the past. He couldn't go and join them. And he couldn't let go of the paper, or it would disappear through the window.

Every now and then, as Molly unwound the roll, there was a little tug. To stop the strip snapping, Davey had to take a step forward. Gradually, he was pulled nearer and nearer the window. He watched anxiously, to see how much further Molly would go.

He was so busy watching Molly that he didn't watch his feet. When he stepped forward again, he put his foot in the waste paper basket and lost his balance. He crashed to the ground, jerking the whole time-line.

Over on the other side of the playground, there was a R-RIP! With a rustle, the paper came curling back through the window, cascading on to Davey's head. Molly roared, and came thundering back across the playground.

"YOU DUMMY! YOU'VE RUINED MY TIME-LINE!"

"That was very careless, Davey,"
said Mrs Johnson, from behind her.
"You ought to make a time-line
yourself. Then you'd see how much
work it takes."

"I –" Davey put a hand into his
pocket and touched the tight little coil
of his own time-line. But he didn't
take it out and show it to Mrs
Johnson. It felt small and silly.

When he got home, he threw it into
his wardrobe.

4. Top Secret!

DAVEY DIDN'T RISK telling anyone about his next idea. Not even Dad, when he phoned from Australia.

"It's a secret."

"A *sea trip*?" said Dad.

"No! A – oh, never mind. I'll tell you when I've finished."

Davey put the phone down and counted his pocket money carefully. He knew just what he was going to do. On Saturday he went into town with Mum and bought three things.

A giant balloon.

A packet of wallpaper paste.

A tin of silver paint.

When he got home, he took a pile of old newspapers up to his bedroom. Then he blew up the balloon and tied a knot in it.

The bedroom door flew open.

"Loon!" said Sarah. "Want loon!"

Davey frowned at her. "Go away."

He put the balloon on top of the wardrobe and went into the bathroom, to mix the wallpaper paste. When he came back, Luke had arrived. He and Sarah were trying to shake the wardrobe, to make the balloon fall down.

Davey pushed them out and shut the door. Then he pulled his armchair across, to stop them getting back in. He needed peace and quiet. He'd made things out of papier mâché before, but only at school.

Slowly and carefully, he tore the

newspaper into strips. He pasted the strips all over the balloon – except at the end, where the knot was. When the layer of paper was thick enough, he put the balloon back on top of the wardrobe.

"What's that?" said Mum, when she came in at bedtime.

"A secret," Davey said.

He didn't tell anyone, even though the papier mâché took a week to dry. And when Molly came round, they stayed in the garden, playing on the climbing frame. Davey wasn't taking any chances.

After a week, the papier mâché was hard. Davey lifted it down from the wardrobe and stuck a pin into the balloon. It collapsed, leaving a shape like a ball with the end chopped off. He put it back on the wardrobe and he went downstairs.

"Have you got an old eggbox, Mum? I need three of those little bobbles that the eggs go in. And a piece of wire."

His mother looked at him. "For your secret?"

"*Maybe*," Davey said carefully.

He glued the eggbox bobbles on to the bottom of the papier mâché, to make three little feet, and bent the

wire into a handle across the opening.
Then he stepped back to look.

It was brilliant. Just like the
cauldrons in the model fort – except
that it was big enough to cook a *real*
soldier's dinner. The only thing wrong
was the colour, and he was going to
change that.

He opened his wardrobe and took
out the tin of silver paint.

By Monday morning, the cauldron
was finished – and it was still a secret.
Davey took it downstairs in a carrier
bag.

Mum grinned. "Do I get a peep?"

Davey almost showed her. Then he
thought, *Suppose she says something when
Molly comes?*

"You can see it tomorrow," he said.

When Molly knocked on the door,
he was standing in the hall with his

coat on, and the bag clutched firmly in both hands.

"What's *that*?" Molly said.

"You'll see," said Davey. "When I show Mrs Johnson."

All the way to school, Molly nagged him to let her see. She promised him a piece of chewing gum. She said she would do all his sums. She even offered to lend him her encyclopaedia. But Davey didn't give in. He held the bag tightly shut, thinking of the beautiful silver cauldron inside.

He and Molly went into the

cloakroom, side by side, and took off
their coats.

"Just a tiny, weeny *peep*?" Molly said.

"No." Davey put the bag on the
floor, behind him, and kept his eye on
Molly. Ready to grab the bag if she
turned round to look in.

But she didn't turn round. What she

did was much worse. When she had
hung up her coat, she took one long,
fast step backwards. Davey didn't have
a chance to move before her foot
came down – CRUNCH! – right on
top of the bag.

"Oh *dear*!" she said.

Davey bent down and pulled out the
cauldron. It was ruined. Molly's foot
had crashed on to it, squashing the
front. No one could possibly have
cooked anything in a cauldron like
that.

Molly peeped over his shoulder. "I
could help you mend it. If you tell me
what it is."

Davey shook his head. Picking
up the bag, he ran out into the
playground. His mother was standing
by the gate, talking. He pushed the
carrier bag into her hand.

"Please – take it home again."

His mother looked at him. Then she
looked at the bag. "Are you going to
show me?"

"Show!" gurgled Luke.

"See! See!" shouted Sarah.

All the other grown-ups turned
round and Davey backed away,
shaking his head. "No. Don't look.
Just – put it in my wardrobe."

He walked slowly back into school.
What was he going to do now?

5. Invasion!

"I CAN'T COME to school yet," Davey said on Tuesday. "Dad said he might phone."

Molly grabbed his arm. "We'll be late for school, dummy."

"I don't care," Davey said, tugging the arm free.

Molly stamped off down the path in a bad temper. She wasn't used to Davey arguing with her. But Dad didn't phone.

At ten to nine, Mum looked up at the kitchen clock. "Look at the *time*! Where's Molly?"

"She came," Davey said. "But I sent her away."

"Why didn't you *tell* me?" shrieked Mum. "Now you're late!"

She threw Luke and Sarah into the buggy, without even taking their bibs off, and made Davey run all the way to school.

"The play – ground will be – empty," panted Mum. "Every – body – will be – inside."

Davey thought so too, but he was wrong. All the other classes had gone in, but Mrs Johnson's class was still outside. Davey stared. Why were they having extra playtime?

He soon found out, when Mrs Johnson sent them in. Their classroom was full. All the children from Mr Morris's class had come in, and they were sitting in *their* chairs. With *their* things.

Molly took one look, and yelled.

"Keep your hands off my work, Sally Jones!"

Sally just laughed. Molly ran across and tried to shake her out of the chair, but it was no use. Sally held on tightly and laughed even more.

People began to get angry. They grabbed their folders. They pushed at the people in the chairs. They shouted. For a moment it looked as if there was going to be a real fight.

Then the bell rang.

Not the electric bell for break, but the big brass bell from Mrs Johnson's shelf. She stood in the doorway and swung it until everyone was quiet.

"Thank you very much, Mr Morris's children," she said. "An excellent invasion. You can go back to your own room now."

Grinning, Mr Morris's class stood up and squeezed out of the room. Molly seized her chair and sat down firmly.

"That was *horrible*!"

Mrs Johnson smiled. "Didn't you like it?"

"No!" Molly said. "I wanted to thump them!"

Mrs Johnson picked up a pen and wrote on the board – *wanted to thump them.* "How did the rest of you feel about being invaded?"

"Furious!" said Amy.

Mrs Johnson wrote *furious* underneath *wanted to thump them.* "What else?"

Suddenly everyone got the idea. Words began flooding out of their mouths: . . . *angry* . . . *they were stealing* . . . *frightened me* . . . Mrs Johnson wrote everything on the board. Then she stood back, and put the pen down.

"Maybe the Ancient Britons felt like you, when they were invaded by the Romans. Pretend you're Ancient Britons, and write a story about the Romans marching into your village."

Molly stopped scowling. "Great!" She took some paper and began to scribble. Davey read the words over her shoulder.

The Romans are wicked and cruel. They

came to our village and burned down all the houses. I had to save everyone.

Was it really like that, Davey wondered? Were all the Romans horrible and ferocious? Or were some of them like that Roman soldier in the museum? Julius Sneezer.

Remembering Julius Sneezer made him grin. He began to write.

We were all in the hut when this Roman soldier barged in. He was a real dummy. He fell over his own sword and his helmet fell off into our corldron. He wasent very braive . . .

Molly leaned over. "That's silly. And you don't spell brave like that." She stretched across and scribbled out the *i*. "You've got cauldron wrong too."

Davey stopped grinning. He made some sentences, using the words on the board. *I was furious. I wanted to thump him.* Then he got stuck.

"Oh Davey," Mrs Johnson said. "Can't you do better than that? Look at Molly. She's written three pages."

"I'm going to take it home and do lots more." Molly smirked at Davey. "I'll come round and read it to you."

She did. She came after tea, when Davey was sitting by the phone, playing shops with Luke and Sarah.

They had packets of things from the kitchen spread out on a box. Molly pushed everything on to the floor, and sat on the box.

"Ready?" she said. "It's really good." She started to read. "*The Romans are wicked and cruel . . .*"

Davey started picking up packets from the floor, but he wasn't quick enough. Sarah got hold of the soap.

She pulled off the paper. "Choc ice!"

"No, Sarah!" Davey tried to grab it. "It's nasty!"

"Don't interrupt," Molly said crossly. "*I had to fight three Romans with my knife . . .*"

Sarah looked down at the soap and pulled a face. "Nasty!" She gave it to Luke and he began to suck it, like a lollipop.

"No!" Davey shouted.

Molly raised her voice. "*I killed five more Romans . . .*"

But she couldn't go on. Luke was sick all over the rest of her sentence. Very bubbly, soapy sick.

Molly jumped up. "You horrible little boy! I'll have to write it all over again!"

She stamped out of the house, and Davey took the soap away from Luke. "Thanks," he said.

He opened the rag drawer to find something to mop up the sick. There was a worn-out towel, tangled up with old tights and bits of string. He started pulling at it.

Then the phone rang.

"Hallo," said Dad's voice. "Sorry I didn't phone this morning. I was travelling to Paris. And – um – making arrangements. Have you had a good day?"

"Oh *yes!*" Davey said. "We were invaded by Romans, and Molly wanted to thump them. She killed three, but Luke was sick on the rest, and –"

"Hang on!" Dad was laughing so much that Davey could hardly work out what he was saying. "Molly *killed three Romans?*"

"Not *real* Romans!" Davey said. "She – oh, let go, Luke!"

Luke was tugging at an old pair of tights, but it was jumbled up with everything else.

"Legs!" he shouted. "Want legs!"

"Let go!" Davey said. "I'll untangle the legs in a minute."

Dad laughed even louder. It was hard to believe he was so far away. "Who's got tangled legs? Another Roman?"

"Of course not!" said Davey. "It's just –"

And then he had his idea.

The tangled tights *did* look like someone's legs. The legs of someone silly enough to fall into a drawer. Maybe a clumsy idiot who'd tripped over his sword . . .

"Never mind the legs," Dad said, "I've got some news –"

59

But Davey couldn't think about anything except legs. "Hang on," he said. Putting down the receiver, he pulled all the rags out of the rag drawer. As he ran through the door, he shouted.

"Mum! Dad's on the phone!"

Then he raced upstairs. He was going to make something brilliant. Just for fun.

6. Julius Sneezer

DAVEY SPENT THE rest of the evening collecting things.

The pyjamas from the rag drawer.

Two old pairs of tights.

A worn out pillow case.

A pile of newspapers.

He'd just piled them up on his bedroom floor, when Molly opened the door, without knocking. She walked straight in.

"I've copied out my story again." She marched over and sat down on his bed. Then she saw the heap on the floor. "What's that rubbish? I'll take it away. Dad's having a bonfire tomorrow."

"No," Davey said quickly. "I want it."

Molly gave him a suspicious look. "Why? What are you doing? Is it something for the Roman Prize?"

"Of course not. I'm – um – playing dustmen."

"*Dustmen?*" Molly shook her head. "You're *mad*, Davey Tilling. I'll read my story to your mum, instead. *She's* got some sense." She bustled off downstairs.

Davey shut his door tight. Then he began. He stuffed the pillow case with newspaper and tied the end shut, to make a head. Then he stuffed the tights, to make two arms and two legs. He was just going to put them together, inside the pyjamas, when he heard Molly coming back.

Quick as a flash, he threw the whole lot on top of the wardrobe.

Molly sailed in, looking smug. "Your mum says my story's *wonderful*. She said I was a clever little girl. And –" Suddenly, she looked up. Her eyes narrowed. "What are *those*?"

Two fat, brown legs were dangling down from the top of the wardrobe.

"They're – er – for keeping out draughts," Davey gabbled. He tugged at the legs, and they fell on his head. "This one goes round the door." Frantically, he pushed it into place. "And this one goes – um – round the hamster's cage. So he doesn't get a cold. Hamsters hate getting colds. When they sneeze, all the food sprays out of their cheek pouches – WHOOOSH! It goes everywhere, and –"

"You *are* mad," Molly said. "I'm going home."

She shook her head and disappeared. Davey sighed with relief, but he didn't go on with his plan. In case she came back. He felt safer making an assault course for his hamster.

When he got home from school next day, he could hardly wait to get back to the legs.

"We aren't doing anything, are we, Mum?" he said. "I need lots of time."

His mother gave him an odd look. "We're not going *out*. Because we're waiting for –"

"Great!"

Davey didn't wait to hear whom they were waiting for. He headed for the stairs. But, as he reached the bottom, there was a yell.

"Legs!"

Luke and Sarah appeared on the landing with one of his pairs of tights. Clutching one leg each and tugging in opposite directions.

"Let *go*!" Davey said.

There was a horrible, tearing sound. The tights came apart in the middle and Luke and Sarah sat down with a bump. When Davey ran upstairs and grabbed the separate legs, they started to wail.

"My *leg*!"

"Wanta *leg*!"

"Oh, Davey!" said Mum. "How could you make them cry? Just when I'm so busy getting ready for –"

"I'm busy too," Davey said crossly. He went into his bedroom and banged the door.

Using the pyjamas, he managed to make all the bits into a body. Rather a strange body. It was very tall, with a floppy head and long thin legs. Laying

it on the bed, Davey took out his felt
pens.

Carefully, he drew a face on the
pillow case head, trying to make it
look like the Roman soldier at the
fort. With a funny little mouth and
great, bushy eyebrows. And a very big
red nose.

When he'd finished, he took lots of things out of his wardrobe.

The T-shirt, in its blue plastic bag.

The broken piece of wood from the onager.

His brown paper time-line.

The cauldron with the squashed side.

Pulling the T-shirt over the dummy's head, he tied it round the middle with a piece of string. Immediately, the dummy looked more like a soldier in a tunic. Especially when he pinned the plastic bag on to its shoulders, hanging down like a cloak.

The piece of broken wood from the onager made a fine sword. Davey used the rest of his tin of paint to paint it silver and fixed it to the dummy's hand with thick rubber bands.

Uncoiling his time-line, he tore it in half and wound the two brown strips

round the dummy's legs, as sandal straps. It looked even better than he'd hoped, but he wouldn't let himself get excited yet. He picked up the cauldron.

Smoothing the squashed side, he cut it out, in a neat, curved rectangle. He glued a strip of paper to the back, to make a handle, and drew a lightning flash on the silver front. It looked just like the shields in the museum.

All he needed now was a helmet.

He picked up the rest of the cauldron and turned it upside-down, pushing it on to the dummy's head. Then he stepped back to look.

And the tall soldier with the funny face stared back at him, smiling. Just like the soldier at the fort.

"Hallo, Julius Sneezer," Davey said softly.

He was going to call Mum to come and see, but *she* called first.

"Davey! Sarah! Luke! You've got a visitor!"

A visitor? But it was nearly bedtime. Who would come round at a time like that?

There was only one person Davey could think of.

Molly!

7. Discovered!

DAVEY GRABBED JULIUS Sneezer and pushed him into the wardrobe. Then he opened the door.

Luke and Sarah burst in.

"Come!"

"Come on, Dayee!"

They bumped into him so hard that he staggered backwards and crashed into the wardrobe. The doors flew open, and Julius Sneezer fell out on top of him. Luke and Sarah shrieked with delight.

"Man!"

"No!" yelled Davey. He picked the

soldier up and held him out of reach.
Where could he hide him?

"Davey!" Mum sounded impatient.
"Where are you?"

Davey pushed Luke and Sarah
towards the door. "Quick. Mum's got
a nice surprise. Go and see."

They looked doubtful, but they
toddled out and slid down the stairs.
As they went into the kitchen, Davey
heard shrieks of glee. Why were they
so pleased to see Molly?

He didn't have time to find out.
Quickly, he crept across the landing,
into the bathroom. As he bolted the
door, he heard footsteps coming
upstairs. Walking towards his
bedroom. He had to hurry. When
Molly found he wasn't there, she
would start banging on the bathroom
door.

Dragging Julius across the

bathroom, Davey pushed him into the
shower cubicle. He hung him up on
the showerhead and slid the doors
shut.

The feet tiptoed out of his bedroom,
stopped by the bathroom door and
went on, into the twins' room. When
the coast was clear, Davey unbolted

the bathroom door and slipped downstairs.

"Yes, Mum?" he said, innocently. "Did you call?"

Mum looked surprised. "Didn't you see him?"

Davey was listening to the footsteps coming out of the twins' bedroom. Heading for the bathroom. "Him?" he said. "What him?"

Before Mum could answer, there was a noise from upstairs. A laugh.

Suddenly, Davey realized who was up there. It wasn't Molly at all. It was –

"Dad!" he shouted. "Dad! I'm down here!"

He raced out of the kitchen just as a familiar figure appeared at the top of the stairs. A tall man with a funny face and big, bushy eyebrows.

"I think I'm going mad," Dad said,

looking down. "There seems to be an Ancient Roman in the shower."

They all had breakfast together. Luke and Sarah sat on Dad's lap, smearing him with porridge and Marmite, and Davey sat beside him, telling the story of Julius Sneezer. All about the trip to the fort. And what had happened to the onager and the time-line and the cauldron.

And all about Molly.

Dad listened to everything, very quietly. Then he said, "You really wanted to win the Roman Prize, didn't you?"

Davey shrugged. "Well, I can't. We're having our Roman feast tomorrow, and that's when we're choosing the winner. But I haven't got anything to take. I haven't even got any food for the feast."

"What's wrong with taking your soldier?" Dad said.

"*Julius Sneezer?*" Davey stared. "But – Molly would laugh."

Mum sat down on the other side of Davey and began spreading honey on a piece of toast. "Does Molly laugh at you a lot?"

"We-ell." Davey hung his head. "She thinks I'm stupid."

Dad and Mum looked at each other. Then Dad said, "Well, it's time Molly found out she was wrong. *I* think your soldier's wonderful. And I bet all your friends will, too."

Davey thought about Jason and Garry. "They might –"

"That's settled then." Mum held out the piece of toast. "Julius Sneezer's going to school tomorrow."

"But I can't just carry him in. He'd look silly."

Dad took the toast and pushed it into Davey's mouth. "Don't talk. Eat that and listen to me. Julius Sneezer's going to school. *And* you're going to have something very special for the feast . . ."

8. The Roman Feast

NEXT MORNING, MOLLY came round
bright and early with a big tin in her
hands. And a big grin on her face.

"*I've* got special Ancient Roman
food for the feast! My mum's made
honey cakes, and stuffed dates and
prawn rissoles. *And* marzipan dormice.
What have you got?"

"Nothing," said Davey.

"Nothing?" Molly looked shocked.
"But we've all got to –"

"My dad's bringing something
later," Davey said.

Molly peeped into the house. "What

about the Roman prize? What are you taking for that?"

"Nothing," said Davey.

"*Nothing?*" Molly opened her eyes wide. "*I've* got my onager and my time-line and my twenty-page story."

"Yes," Davey said. "I know." He picked up his coat. "Mum! Molly's here!"

Mum came bustling out of the kitchen, drying her hands. "Let's go then. Thank goodness we haven't got to take the twins. They're upstairs with Dad, eating chocolate biscuits in bed."

Molly looked disapproving. "My mum never lets *me* eat in bed. She says it's too messy."

"You poor little thing," said Davey's mum.

Molly was so surprised that she didn't say another word, all the way to school.

Davey felt very strange that
morning. He was the only person who
hadn't brought anything. Everyone
else was busy getting the feast ready
and arranging models on the display
table. There were three or four
onagers, six time-lines and lots of
swords. Jason and Garry had drawn a
plan of the Roman fort, and Amy had

made a Roman dress for her Sindy doll.

But no one had made as much as Molly. She spent the morning looking smug and pretending to be modest.

"I'm not really the best," she kept saying. "Everyone else has tried *very hard*. Amy's Roman dress is lovely. Even if she has got it wrong. And Leo's onager is just as good as mine. Except that it doesn't work."

Davey didn't say a word. But he kept thinking, *Please don't let Dad forget.*

Dad didn't. At break, as they were all going into the playground, Davey saw their big blue car drive past, into the teachers' car park. He grinned. But he didn't say a word.

When they went back in after break, their classroom was ready for the feast. All the tables were stacked on one side of the room, and the curtain was pulled across the end, shutting off the book corner.

Mrs Johnson had made a big low table with the staging from the hall. It was covered with a white cloth, and all the food was spread out on top. Honey cakes and prawn rissoles. Marzipan dormice and stuffed dates. Little brown biscuits, bowls of lentils and boiled eggs with a strange-looking sauce. There was even a big jug of blackcurrant, pretending to be wine.

"We'll lie down to eat," Mrs Johnson said. "That's what the Romans did."

"Yes!" said Jason. "Like eating in bed!"

Molly pulled a face, but no one took any notice. They were too busy looking at the food. Except for Davey. He was staring at the curtain that shut off the book corner. *I hope it's going to be all right*, he thought.

"What about the competition?" Molly said loudly. "When are we going to choose the winner?"

"In a minute," Mrs Johnson said. "But before we vote, there's someone I want you to see." She smiled at Davey and marched across to the book corner. "Meet Julius Sneezer!"

With a flourish, she pulled back the curtain – and there was Julius, hanging straight and tall on the cupboard door, with a biscuit tin at his feet.

Everyone gasped. Then they started to laugh and cheer.

"Brilliant!" said Garry.

"Did you make him, Miss?" said Jason.

"I want him to sit next to *me*," said Amy.

Mrs Johnson smiled again. "*I* didn't make him. Davey did. He's been working on him ever since we went to the Roman fort, haven't you, Davey?"

"Sort of," said Davey. "I –"

He didn't get a chance to explain. Garry spun round and slapped him on the back.

"You're the winner! You've got to be."

Everyone started chanting it. "The winner! The winner!"

The only person not chanting was Molly. She stood by the curtain, glaring at Julius Sneezer. When the shouting died down, she sidled up to Mrs Johnson.

"It's not fair," she said. "*I* thought we had to make the things by ourselves. Davey couldn't have done that on his own. Someone must have helped him."

Mrs Johnson looked at her. "I don't think so, Molly. Davey's father told me

all about it. You didn't have any help,
did you, Davey?"

Davey looked at Julius Sneezer.
Then he looked at Molly. He had
never seen her so miserable and cross.

"I didn't have any *help*," he said
slowly. "But I couldn't have done it
without –"

Everyone was staring at him, but he
was determined to finish.

"I couldn't have done it without *you*, Molly."

Molly went bright scarlet. Suddenly, Davey felt sorry for her. It was a very strange feeling. Bending down, he picked up the biscuit tin that was lying at Julius Sneezer's feet.

"Here," he said. "Have one of these. My dad made them specially for the feast."

He pulled the lid off the tin and Molly peered in suspiciously.

"What are they?"

Davey managed not to smile. "Rhubarb pies," he said.

Choosing a brilliant book
can be a tricky business...
but not any more

www.puffin.co.uk

The best selection of books at your fingertips

So get clicking!

Searching the site is easy – you'll find
what you're looking for at the click of a mouse,
from great authors to brilliant books and more!

Read more in Puffin

For complete information about books available from Puffin – and Penguin – and how to order them, contact us at the appropriate address below. Please note that for copyright reasons the selection of books varies from country to country.

www.puffin.co.uk

In the United Kingdom: Please write to Dept EP, Penguin Books Ltd, Bath Road, Harmondsworth, West Drayton, Middlesex UB7 ODA

In the United States: Please write to Penguin Putnam Inc., P.O. Box 12289, Dept B, Newark, New Jersey 07101–5289 or call 1–800–788–6262

In Canada: Please write to Penguin Books Canada Ltd, 10 Alcorn Avenue, Suite 300, Toronto, Ontario M4V 3B2

In Australia: Please write to Penguin Books Australia Ltd, P.O. Box 257, Ringwood, Victoria 3134

In New Zealand: Please write to Penguin Books (NZ) Ltd, Private Bag 102902, North Shore Mail Centre, Auckland 10

In India: Please write to Penguin Books India Pvt Ltd, 11 Panscheel Shopping Centre, Panscheel Park, New Delhi 110 017

In the Netherlands: Please write to Penguin Books Netherlands bv, Postbus 3507, NL–1001 AH Amsterdam

In Germany: Please write to Penguin Books Deutschland GmbH, Metzlerstrasse 26, 60594 Frankfurt am Main

In Spain: Please write to Penguin Books S. A., Bravo Murillo 19, 1° B, 28015 Madrid

In Italy: Please write to Penguin Italia s.r.l., Via Felice Casati 20, I–20124 Milano

In France: Please write to Penguin France S. A., 17 rue Lejeune, F–31000 Toulouse

In Japan: Please write to Penguin Books Japan, Ishikiribashi Building, 2–5–4, Suido, Bunkyo-ku, Tokyo 112

In South Africa: Please write to Longman Penguin Southern Africa (Pty) Ltd, Private Bag X08, Bertsham 2013